A Free

A book can shift your perspective, but a ritual can transform your life. As a thank-you for reading, I'd like to offer you our exclusive *Zen Clarity Kit*, designed to help you clear your mind, refocus, and make Zen teachings a part of your daily routine.

What's Inside the Kit?

✓ **The Zen Morning Ritual Guide** – A simple daily practice to anchor your mind in stillness.

✓ **A 5-Minute Audio Meditation** – Gently guide yourself into a state of clarity and focus.

✓ **Zen Minimalism Wallpapers** – Subtle reminders to cultivate presence throughout your day.

>> Scan the QR Code or click here to download your free gift <<

Table of Contents

Introduction

What Is Beauty?

What makes something beautiful?

Is it symmetry? Perfection? A flawless surface without cracks or imperfections?

Or could beauty be found in the worn edges of an old book, the uneven glaze of a handmade cup, or the golden lines of a mended bowl?

We are taught to seek perfection—to smooth out the rough spots, to hide the flaws, to become polished and whole. But Zen teaches us a different way: that true beauty lies not in perfection, but in authenticity. It's the crack, not the smooth surface, that makes something unique.

Imagine holding a broken cup. At first, you see only the damage—the sharp edges, the missing piece. But what if you filled the cracks with gold? The cup would not be perfect, but it would be more beautiful for having been broken and made whole again.

This is where Zen comes in.

Zen isn't about creating a perfect life. It's about learning to see the beauty in what's already here—even the cracks. It's about accepting imperfection, releasing self-judgment, and discovering that peace isn't found in flawless outcomes—it's found in loving what is incomplete.

What Are Zen Stories?

Think about the last time you saw beauty in something unexpected—a faded photograph, the sound of rain on a window, the quiet strength of someone letting go. Some truths don't arrive through explanations—they arrive through experience.

Zen stories are like that. They don't explain. They reveal.

Instead of telling you what to think, Zen stories invite you to see things differently. Sometimes they're simple. Sometimes they're strange. Sometimes they make no sense at all—until, suddenly, they do.

A Zen master once said, "The broken pot holds more light." Meaning? The flaws, the imperfections—these are not signs of failure. They are openings for grace.

Zen stories are reminders. They help you stop striving, stop fixing, and start seeing the quiet perfection in the imperfect. They teach you that true peace isn't in being whole—it's in being real.

This book is a collection of **21 Zen stories**, each one designed to help you soften the harsh edges of self-judgment and see the quiet beauty in life's imperfect moments.

How Do I Use This Book?

First rule: There are no rules.

Read this book however you want. Open it randomly, read one story a day, or finish it in one sitting. There's no perfect way to experience Zen.

But if you'd like a suggestion—try reading one story a day for 21 days. Let it sit with you. Don't rush to understand it. Just let the story unfold naturally in your mind. Some will make sense immediately. Others might confuse you. That's part of the process.

After each story, you'll find a simple reflection —a thought, a question, or a small practice to try in your own life. You don't have to "figure it out." Just let the ideas settle, like gold finding its place in a cracked bowl.

Because the truth is, you don't have to be flawless to be whole.

You just have to let yourself be seen.

— *Kai*

PART I
The Weight of Wanting

TO SEEK IS TO SUFFER. TO SEEK
NOTHING IS BLISS.

Buddha

1

THE MAN WHO OWNED THE MOON

THE RICHEST MAN IN THE PROVINCE
stood at the edge of his garden, gazing into his

pond. The full moon shimmered upon the surface, trembling with every ripple. He had spent a lifetime accumulating wealth—golden statues, silk tapestries, ivory carvings—but no possession enchanted him like this.

"I must own it," he whispered.

The next morning, he summoned his servants. "Find a way to capture the moon in my pond," he commanded. "I will reward the one who succeeds."

His most trusted builder erected tall stone walls around the pond, shielding it from the wind so the moon's reflection would remain undisturbed. But the walls darkened the water, and the moon vanished.

A scholar suggested draining the pond and sealing the reflection in a great mirror. But once the water was gone, the moon was gone too.

A fisherman, desperate for reward, cast a great net upon the pond. He pulled it in, only to find it empty, dripping silver in the moonlight.

The rich man grew furious. "Useless, all of you! The moon is there every night, yet none of you can grasp it!"

An old monk passing through the village overheard the commotion. He stepped forward, gazing into the pond. "You wish to own the moon?" he asked.

The rich man scoffed. "Can you do better than these fools?"

The monk knelt at the edge of the pond, cupped his hands, and gently lifted a pool of water. The moon's reflection shimmered in his palms. "Here," he said, holding it out. "Take it."

The rich man reached out eagerly, but as soon as he touched the water, it slipped through his fingers. The ripples scattered the moonlight. He stared at his empty hands.

The monk simply turned and walked away, leaving the rich man staring into the pond, his own reflection rippling alongside the moon's.

For a long time, the man stood motionless, watching as the moon danced freely over the water. That night, he lay awake, unable to stop thinking about what had slipped through his grasp.

The next evening, he returned to the pond, but this time, he did not try to capture the moon. He simply watched.

Reflection

**What in your life do you chase,
not realizing you already have it?**

**How does the act of grasping change what
we seek?**

―――

A Moment of Zen

Hold a bowl of water.
Watch how light moves upon its surface.

Open your hand, then slowly close it.
Feel the difference between holding and
letting go.

Step outside and look at the moon.
Ask yourself: *Who owns this?*

2

THE FARMER'S MISSING PIECE

A FARMER HAD THE MOST PROSPEROUS
land in the valley, yet he was never satisfied.

Each season, he sought to improve his fields—plowing deeper, planting new crops, building higher fences. Still, he felt something was missing.

One day, he visited an old sage in the mountains. "I have everything," the farmer said, "but I still feel incomplete. What am I missing?"

The sage smiled and handed the farmer a simple wooden bowl. "Fill this with the perfect grain, and your question will be answered."

The farmer traveled far and wide, selecting the finest grains—golden wheat, fragrant rice, rare barley—but each time he placed one in the bowl, another would roll out. He adjusted, replaced, and rearranged, but the bowl was never full.

Frustrated, he returned to the sage. "I have searched everywhere, yet I cannot fill this bowl."

The sage only smiled and gestured to the bowl. The farmer, watching a single grain roll to the edge but never quite falling, suddenly understood.

Sitting quietly, he turned the bowl in his hands. He thought of his fields, his crops, and the endless search for more. He had plowed deeper, planted wider, and yet, the feeling of lack had never faded. Perhaps it had nothing to do with the land after all.

Returning home, he placed the bowl on his table, no longer needing to fill it. When harvest time came, he did not count his yield—he simply gathered what was before him, and for the first time, it was enough.

Reflection

Where in your life do you feel incomplete, and why?

What happens when you stop trying to 'fill' what is already whole?

———

A Moment of Zen

Hold an empty cup in your hands. Notice how it is both full of space and empty of substance.

Gather small objects and place them in a bowl. Observe what stays and what falls away.

Walk through a field or garden and find a single blade of grass. Ask yourself: *Is this enough?*

3

THE MERCHANT WHO SOLD EMPTINESS

A TRAVELING MERCHANT ARRIVED IN A
bustling town, setting up his stall in the mar-

ketplace. He laid out his wares—silks, spices, and rare trinkets—but his most prized item was an empty wooden box.

Curious townsfolk gathered. "What is in the box?" a woman asked.

"Emptiness," the merchant replied with a smile. "And for a price, it can be yours."

The people laughed. "Who would buy nothing?" they scoffed.

Yet, as the day passed, whispers spread. A scholar approached. "True emptiness is priceless," he mused, and he paid for the box, carrying it away with reverence.

By sunset, the merchant had sold every box. When the townspeople returned, hoping to buy one, they found only an empty stall.

Confused, they asked, "Where is the merchant?"

A child pointed to the horizon, where a lone figure disappeared into the fading light, carrying nothing at all. And for the first time, they began to wonder if perhaps they, too, already possessed what he had been selling all along.

Reflection

What value do you place on emptiness in your life?

How does space—whether in your mind, home, or heart—create opportunity?

———

A Moment of Zen

Sit in an empty room and observe how it feels.

Hold an open container in your hands. What gives it purpose—the structure or the space inside?

Let go of one thought you've been holding onto.
Notice what remains.

4

THE GOLD THAT MELTED IN THE RAIN

THE STORM RAGED THROUGH THE
night, rattling the rooftops and flooding the

BEAUTY IN THE ZEN

streets. By dawn, the rain had stopped, leaving behind broken branches and pools of muddy water. Hiroshi stepped outside and gasped—his prized golden statues, the secret vault of his wealth, had been reduced to formless lumps.

A wealthy merchant, Hiroshi, possessed an immense fortune but was plagued by the fear of thieves. Wary of banks and hidden vaults, he devised a plan—he commissioned a sculptor to mold his gold into life-sized statues, placing them in his garden as if they were mere decorations.

Visitors marveled at the craftsmanship, never suspecting that the statues were not merely gilded but pure gold. Hiroshi took pride in his deception, believing he had outwitted greed itself. His sculptures stood in the village square, admired by all, yet no one knew their true worth.

One evening, dark clouds gathered over the town, and the heavens opened. A heavy rain poured through the night, soaking the earth and flooding the streets. When dawn broke, Hiroshi stepped into his garden and gasped in horror. The statues—once solid and magnificent—had softened, their edges crumbling.

Gold, so pure it had been malleable, had washed away in streams of glittering mud.

Hiroshi knelt before the crumbling statues, his hands coated in golden dust, watching helplessly as the rain carried his life's work into the earth. His neighbors gathered in silence, watching his despair.

An old monk, who often passed through the town, stepped forward. He examined the ruined garden, then picked up a handful of golden dust, letting it slip through his fingers. "Strange," he murmured, "how something so valuable disappears the moment we try to keep it."

Hiroshi stared at the empty pedestals, realizing that in his effort to preserve his fortune, he had lost both the art and the gold. The wealth had never truly been his—only borrowed for a time, like everything else in life.

That night, as the rain began to fall again, Hiroshi sat in his empty workshop, no longer weighing his success in gold, but in the memories of what his hands had once shaped.

Reflection

What do you hold onto so tightly that it controls you?

If everything you owned washed away tomorrow, what would remain?

———

A Moment of Zen

Stand in the rain and feel the weight of your worries dissolve.

Let go of a handful of sand or soil. Watch how the wind or water takes it.

Watch water flow down a street. Reflect on how all things eventually return to the earth.

5

THE MASON AND THE BOULDER

THE MASON WIPED HIS BROW AND
pressed his hands against the boulder. For

years, this giant stone had blocked the village road, forcing travelers to take the long way around. The villagers had long since accepted it, but today, the mason decided to move it.

A mason named Ryuu returned home after years of work in a distant city. At the entrance, he found this massive boulder blocking the path. The villagers walked around it each day, grumbling at its presence but making no effort to move it.

Seeing an obstacle where others saw a nuisance, Ryuu stepped forward. He placed his hands upon the rough surface and heaved with all his might. It barely budged. Yet, undeterred, he tried again and again.

The villagers stopped to watch, curious but unconvinced. "Why waste your energy?" they said. "The boulder has always been here."

At last, with one final heave, Ryuu felt the stone shift. Beneath it, he discovered a small hollow filled with gold coins and a note that read: *He who makes the path easier for others is rewarded beyond measure.*

The villagers gasped, realizing they had walked past this hidden treasure every day. Ryuu knelt, picked up a single coin, and left the rest behind.

As he walked away, a young boy ran after him and asked, "Why take only one?"

Ryuu chuckled. "Because I have all that I need."

Reflection

What obstacles in your life might be hiding opportunities?

How does effort shape the way we perceive value?

———

A Moment of Zen

Find a rock and move it from one place to another.
Reflect on the effort it takes.

Observe a path you walk often—
what have you never noticed before?

Ask yourself: *What do I truly need?*

PART II
The Beauty of the Unfinished

To be beautiful means to be yourself. You don't need to be accepted by others. You need to accept yourself.

Thich Nhat Hanh

6

THE CRACKED TEA CUP

THE YOUNG MONK, RIKU, WAS
sweeping the temple courtyard when his sleeve

brushed against the tea table. A delicate porcelain cup wobbled, then tumbled to the stone floor. It shattered into five jagged pieces.

Riku froze. His master, old and serene, had been drinking from that cup for years.

Heart pounding, he gathered the fragments in his hands and hurried inside. "Master," he said, his voice tight with regret. "I have broken your cup."

The master glanced at the pieces, then nodded. "So you have."

Riku lowered his head. "Shall I throw it away?"

The old man chuckled. "Why would you do that? It is not dead—it is simply waiting to be made whole again."

That afternoon, the master guided Riku to a small box in the temple storehouse. Inside was a jar of golden lacquer. "We will mend it," he said.

With careful hands, they fit the pieces together, filling each crack with shimmering gold. When the lacquer dried, the cup gleamed—not perfect as before, but even more beautiful.

Riku traced the golden lines with his fingertip. "But the cracks still show."

The master smiled. "Yes. Now they are part of its story."

That evening, the master poured tea into the cup once more. As the steam curled into the air, Riku realized—this cup was not ruined. It was transformed.

Reflection

When something breaks in your life, do you see it as the end, or a chance to repair?

Can flaws and imperfections hold their own kind of beauty?

A Moment of Zen

Take something broken and mend it with care.
Notice how it changes.

Observe a scar on your body.
Reflect on the story it carries.

Pour tea into a cup and watch the steam rise.
Ask yourself: *What has been reshaped within me?*

7

THE RIVER THAT WROTE POEMS

A POET SAT BY THE RIVERBANK, watching the current carry fallen leaves downstream. With each passing moment, he felt words rise within him—verses forming and dissolving like ripples on the water's surface.

Inspired, he took a thin reed and dipped it into the river, trying to write his poem directly upon the flowing water. The ink dispersed instantly, his words vanishing as soon as they appeared.

A fisherman nearby chuckled. "What are you doing?"

"I am writing poetry," the poet replied.

"But nothing remains," the fisherman said.

"Perhaps that is the most honest poem of all," the poet mused. "Each word is here for a moment, then gone, like everything else."

The fisherman thought for a while, then cast his line into the river. "Then I suppose fishing is a poem as well. You drop the hook, you wait, and sometimes, you catch something—but mostly, you just watch the water."

The poet smiled. He set down his reed, closed his eyes, and listened to the river's endless verses, spoken without a single word.

Reflection

What do you create or pursue that is meant to last? What if it didn't need to?

How does impermanence shape the meaning of our efforts?

———

A Moment of Zen

Watch a river or stream and observe how it moves without clinging to anything.

Drop a leaf into flowing water and watch where it goes.

Sit quietly and listen to the sounds around you.
Notice how they arise and fade away.

8

THE PAINTING THAT WAS NEVER SIGNED

IN THE HEART OF A BUSTLING CITY, there was an artist named Renji, known for his breathtaking landscapes. Collectors sought his work, nobles displayed his paintings in their halls, and students traveled miles to learn from him. Yet, there was one painting that no one had ever seen completed.

For *forty years*, Renji worked on the same canvas. It sat in his studio, a masterpiece in progress. Every day, he adjusted a stroke, softened a shadow, or deepened a color. His students whispered about it, calling it *the perfect painting*. But no one ever saw it finished.

One evening, an eager student gathered the courage to ask, "Master, when will the painting be complete?"

Renji smiled, setting down his brush. "Perhaps tomorrow. Perhaps never."

Years passed. The student became an artist in his own right, yet the thought of Renji's unfinished masterpiece never left him. One day, he returned to his old teacher's studio and found it empty—Renji had passed away.

The famous painting still stood on its easel, untouched. The student stepped forward, eager to finally see it. But when he pulled away the cloth, he gasped.

The canvas was **almost empty**—just a few strokes of sky, a suggestion of a mountain, and the faint curve of a river.

Confused, he turned to an old note Renji had left behind:

"A painting is never complete. The moment we think it is, it ceases to be alive."

Reflection

**Where in your life do you seek perfection?
What happens if you stop?**

**Can something be complete
without being finished?**

———

A Moment of Zen

Start a drawing, then stop before you feel it's
done.
Observe how it feels.

Write a sentence, then remove the last word.
See if it still speaks.

Watch a sunset and notice that its beauty lies
in its fading.

9

THE TEMPLE THAT WASHES AWAY

BY THE EDGE OF THE SEA, A SMALL
village built a temple to honor the tides. Every

plank was carved by hand, every stone placed with care. The villagers came daily to offer incense, bowing before the waves that never ceased their rhythm.

A young monk, Daiki, tended the temple. One morning, as he swept the steps, he saw an old man watching the horizon. "What do you see?" Daiki asked.

"The sea is patient," the old man said. "But one day, it will take this temple back."

Daiki frowned. "We have worked so hard to build this place. Why would the sea take it?"

The old man chuckled. "Because that is its nature."

Years passed. The temple stood through storms and seasons. But one night, the sea rose higher than before. Waves crashed against the wooden pillars, pulling them into the tide. By morning, nothing remained but the wet sand.

The villagers wept. "All our work—washed away in a single night!"

But Daiki did not mourn. Instead, he took a piece of driftwood from the shore and began carving. When the villagers asked what he was doing, he smiled.

"We build, the sea takes. Then we build again."

And so, the temple was rebuilt.

Reflection

**What in your life do you try to make permanent,
even though it cannot last?**

**How do you respond when something you
built is taken away?**

––––––

A Moment of Zen

Stack stones by the water,
then watch the tide return them to the earth.

Place one stone on another,
then let them fall and rebuild it again.

Watch a wave rise and fall.
Ask yourself: *Is it ever truly gone?*

10

THE MELTING SNOWFLAKE

SNOWFLAKES TUMBLED FROM THE SKY, settling softly on the ground. Haru ran through the winter fields, his breath rising in small clouds. He held out his hands, catching the delicate flakes, marveling at their perfect, intricate patterns.

"Look how perfect they are!" he exclaimed to his grandfather, who stood nearby, watching.

His grandfather chuckled. "Yes, but look again."

Haru peered into his palm. The snowflake, once intricate and whole, was already dissolving. The warmth of his skin had melted it into a single drop of water.

Frowning, Haru wiped his hand against his coat. "Why do they disappear so fast?"

His grandfather placed his hand on Haru's shoulder. "Nothing stays as it is, Haru. But that doesn't mean it's lost."

"But I wanted to keep it," the boy said, glancing up at the gray sky.

The old man scooped up a handful of snow and patted it into a ball. "Then hold onto this instead."

Haru took the snowball, feeling its weight in his hands. But as they walked home, he noticed something—bit by bit, the ball was shrinking, water seeping through his fingers.

By the time they reached the house, nothing remained but the coldness in his palm. He sighed.

His grandfather only smiled. "See? You never lost it. It just changed."

Haru stared at his empty hands for a long moment. Then, he ran back outside and lifted his face to the falling snow, laughing as the flakes landed on his skin, melting instantly.

Reflection

**Have you ever tried to capture a moment,
only to find it slipping away?**

**If something is always changing,
does that mean it's gone?**

———

A Moment of Zen

Catch a snowflake in your hand.
Watch how it melts.

Hold a piece of ice, then let it return to water.
Feel it change.

Watch the clouds drift across the sky.
Do they ever truly vanish?

PART III
The Lightness of Letting Go

To hold on is to be serious;
to let go is to lighten.

Zen Proverb

11

THE LADDER TO THE SKY

FOR YEARS, A DEVOTED MONK NAMED
Jiro sought enlightenment. He meditated in

the mountains, fasted for days, and read every sacred text. Yet, the truth he sought always seemed just out of reach.

One morning, he awoke with a revelation. "I must climb higher," he thought. "Enlightenment must be above me."

So he built a ladder.

At dawn, he climbed to the first rung, then the second. He meditated there, expecting to feel wiser. But he was no different than before. So he climbed higher.

Days turned to weeks, and Jiro's ladder stretched above the village, above the trees, even above the clouds. He barely ate or slept, only climbing, always higher.

One day, as he reached for the next rung, he heard laughter below. He looked down and saw his old master sitting beneath the ladder, drinking tea.

"Master!" Jiro called. "I am close to enlightenment! Just a little higher!"

The old man sipped his tea. "Oh? And where does the ladder end?"

Jiro looked up. His ladder disappeared into the endless blue sky. He had never considered this. Where *did* it end?

For the first time in years, he hesitated. The sky stretched infinitely above him. His legs trembled. He had no idea what he was climbing toward.

Slowly, carefully, he climbed back down.

When he reached the ground, his master handed him a cup of tea. Jiro sat, breathing in the steam, feeling the earth beneath him.

The old man chuckled. "If the sky has no top, where do you think enlightenment is hiding?"

Jiro took a sip of tea. It was the best tea he had ever tasted.

Reflection

**What goals in your life feel like a ladder
with no top?**

**Are you chasing something distant while
ignoring what's already in your hands?**

———

A Moment of Zen

Climb a small hill, then sit at the top.
Observe what changes.

Pour a cup of tea and drink it slowly.
Notice if you are truly present.

Look at the sky. Ask yourself:
Where does it begin? Where does it end?

12

THE BOOK WITH THE MISSING PAGE

IN A QUIET MONASTERY, THERE WAS A single book that all the monks studied. Its pages were filled with wisdom—poems, parables, and teachings passed down for generations.

Late one night, a young monk named Taro was reading this book when he noticed something strange. A page was missing.

Alarmed, he rushed to his master. "Master, the book is incomplete! A page has been lost!"

The master smiled. "Ah, yes. That page was missing when I was your age as well."

Taro frowned. "But what if it contained something important?"

The old man shrugged. "Then perhaps you must discover it for yourself."

Taro was unsatisfied. He searched the monastery, questioned the elders, and even tried to rewrite the missing page from memory —but he could never be certain what had been lost.

One evening, as he sat by the lantern light, staring at the gap in the book, a thought arose: *Why do I assume the missing page was more important than the ones still here?*

The next morning, he returned to his master. "I have studied every page, yet the missing one still lingers in my mind."

The master chuckled. "And what have you learned?"

Taro hesitated, then said, "That sometimes, an unanswered question is the most valuable lesson of all."

The master nodded. "Perhaps that missing page was the most important one after all."

Taro smiled. He never searched for it again.

Reflection

What unanswered questions in your life do you struggle to let go of?

Can uncertainty itself be a teacher?

———

A Moment of Zen

Read a passage in a book, then stop before the last sentence. Notice how it feels.

Sit in silence and listen to the silence between sounds.

Write a question on a piece of paper, then fold it away without answering it.

13

THE SOUND OF ONE HAND

TETSU HAD LIVED IN THE MONASTERY
since childhood, sweeping the halls and

copying sutras by candlelight. Though years had passed, enlightenment still eluded him. One evening, as the lanterns flickered in the temple hall, he approached his master.

"Master," Tetsu said, bowing deeply, "I have read every sutra, memorized every teaching, and yet I still do not understand. What is the true nature of Zen?"

The master sipped his tea in silence. Then, without looking up, he said, "Tell me, what is the sound of one hand clapping?"

Tetsu straightened. "That is a famous koan, Master. But I do not know the answer."

The old man nodded. "Good. Come back when you do."

For weeks, Tetsu meditated on the question. He clapped his hands together, then tried waving one in the air. He listened to the wind, the rustling leaves, even the hush of falling snow. Each time, he returned to his master with an answer.

"The wind in the trees?"

"No."

"The hush of silence?"

"No."

"The absence of sound?"

The master only smiled.

One morning, exhausted, Tetsu sat by the temple pond, watching the ripples spread. A frog leapt into the water, sending waves in all directions. He took a deep breath. There it was.

That evening, he returned to his master. He bowed and raised his hand in silence.

The master chuckled and poured him a cup of tea. "Now, you are beginning to hear."

Reflection

Are some questions meant to be answered, or simply experienced?

How do you listen—to words, to silence, to the space in between?

_____

A Moment of Zen

Sit in a quiet room. Pay attention not to the sounds, but to the silence between them.

Place your hand in water, then lift it. Notice the ripples that remain.

Clap your hands, then hold one still. Ask yourself: *What remains?*

14

THE HOUSE MADE OF ASH

A WIDOW NAMED EMIKO LIVED IN A small wooden house at the edge of the village.

For years, she had built a quiet life there, tending to her garden and sweeping the floors each morning. She owned little, but every object had a story—a worn silk robe from her mother, a clay teapot gifted by a dear friend, an old flute her husband had once played.

One summer, a terrible fire swept through the village. The wind carried embers from rooftop to rooftop, and the sky burned red through the night. The villagers threw buckets of water, shouting and scrambling, but the flames moved faster than their hands.

By morning, Emiko's house was gone—nothing remained but blackened beams and drifting ash.

The villagers gathered to comfort her. "You have lost everything," they said.

Emiko bent down and picked up a handful of ash. It slipped through her fingers, carried away by the wind. She watched it swirl into the sky, then smiled.

"No," she said softly. "I have only lost what could burn."

The villagers exchanged puzzled looks.

She walked toward the ruins of her home, stepping over the charred remains of her teapot and the ashes where her flute had once rested. But instead of weeping, she knelt and placed her hands on the ground.

"This," she said, patting the warm earth, "has not burned."

And with that, she stood and began gathering stones for a new foundation.

Reflection

What in your life feels permanent, yet could disappear in an instant?

When faced with loss, do you mourn, rebuild, or something else?

A Moment of Zen

Burn a small piece of paper and watch the ash scatter.
What is left behind?

Sit in a quiet room and notice what is *not* there.

Touch the ground beneath you and ask yourself: *What did it used to be?*

15

THE UNCARVED BLOCK

IN A QUIET MOUNTAIN VILLAGE, AN
elderly woodcarver named Sora was known for

his intricate sculptures. His hands, weathered by decades of work, could shape wood into life-like animals, flowing rivers, and even the delicate folds of a monk's robe.

One day, a young apprentice arrived at his workshop, eager to learn. "Master," he said, "what is the most difficult thing to carve?"

Sora placed his hand on an untouched block of wood. "This."

The apprentice frowned. "But it is nothing yet."

Sora smiled. "Exactly."

For weeks, the apprentice watched as the master carved. Each piece took shape with effortless precision, yet the untouched block remained in the corner. One day, curiosity overtook him. "Master, why haven't you carved that block?"

Sora ran his fingers along the grain of the wood. "Because not everything must be shaped. Sometimes, the greatest beauty is in what is left untouched."

The apprentice struggled with this idea. He

spent years trying to master the perfect carving, but the block in the corner remained as it was.

When Sora passed away, the villagers gathered to honor him. The apprentice, now grown, stood in the workshop. He looked at the unfinished wood, then ran his hands along its surface, just as his master once had.

For the first time, he saw the lines of the grain, the knots and swirls, the quiet perfection of what had never been altered.

And so, he placed the block on the altar—uncarved, as it had always been.

Reflection

Do we improve everything by shaping it, or is there value in leaving some things untouched?

Where in your life do you try to change what is already whole?

———

A Moment of Zen

Hold an unsharpened pencil or a blank sheet of paper. Notice its potential without altering it.

Find a natural object—a stone, a leaf, a piece of wood. Observe it without changing it.

Sit in stillness.
Ask yourself: *What if nothing needed fixing?*

PART IV
Loving Without Holding

IF YOU LOVE A FLOWER, DON'T
PICK IT. IF YOU PICK IT, IT DIES,
AND IT CEASES TO BE WHAT YOU
LOVE. SO IF YOU LOVE A FLOWER,
LET IT BE.

Osho

16

THE GARDEN THAT GREW WILD

THE GOVERNOR'S GARDEN WAS THE pride of the province. A place of perfect symmetry—each tree pruned to precise angles, each stone carefully placed, every flower arranged in neat, orderly rows. For twenty years, the gardener, Naoki, had tended it with unwavering devotion.

In the middle of the night, a storm rampaged through the village. The winds howled through the garden, tearing petals from their stems and uprooting the smaller shrubs. Rain battered the soil, turning the paths into streams of mud. When the skies cleared, Naoki surveyed the wreckage in horror. His perfect garden was ruined.

But before he could begin replanting, the governor arrived.

Naoki bowed low. "I will restore everything at once, my lord."

The governor studied the tangled vines, the wild scatter of blossoms, the branches swaying freely in the wind. Then he smiled. "No," he said. "For the first time, the garden is alive."

Naoki hesitated. He had spent his life imposing order upon this land, yet now, in its untamed state, something stirred within him. He knelt and ran his hands through the damp earth, watching as a single butterfly landed on an untrimmed branch.

That spring, he did not cut the grass too short. He let the wildflowers bloom where they pleased. The trees grew as they wished, their branches stretching freely toward the sky.

And for the first time, Naoki felt at peace.

Reflection

Where in your life do you try to impose control
instead of allowing things to grow naturally?

Can something be more beautiful when left
untamed?

———

A Moment of Zen

Let a plant grow without trimming or
shaping it. Observe how it finds its own way.

Sit in a field or forest. Notice how nature
arranges itself without interference.

Pour water onto the ground and watch how
it flows.
Ask yourself: *Does it resist?*

17

THE BUTTERFLY THAT WAS NEVER CAUGHT

HIRO HAD SPENT HIS LIFE STUDYING beauty. As a scholar of nature, he traveled across mountains and valleys, cataloging rare flowers, sketching the perfect curve of a bird's wing, and measuring the patterns on fallen leaves. He believed that if he observed carefully enough, he would one day understand the secret behind all things beautiful.

One afternoon, while walking through a meadow, he spotted a butterfly—its wings shimmering blue and gold in the sunlight. "This," he thought, "is the most perfect creature I have ever seen."

He reached for it, but the butterfly fluttered away.

Determined to study it up close, Hiro followed. Through fields and over hills, he chased the delicate creature, adjusting his steps to match its erratic flight. Yet, each time he neared, it slipped just beyond his grasp.

Finally, exhausted, he collapsed beneath a tree. His breath was heavy, his hands empty.

And then, as the wind settled, the butterfly circled back. It drifted gently through the air and landed on his open palm.

Hiro held his breath, afraid to move. The butterfly rested for a moment, then lifted off again, disappearing into the golden light.

He sat there, watching the empty space where it had been, and smiled.

Some things, he realized, could only be seen when left to be free.

Reflection

**What happens when you stop chasing
and simply stand still?**

**How does holding on too tightly
change what we love?**

————

A Moment of Zen

Hold out your hand and let something rest
on it—a leaf, a petal, a feather. Notice when it
chooses to leave.

Watch a bird in flight. Observe how it moves
without force or direction.

Sit in stillness and ask yourself:
What comes to me when I stop chasing?

18

THE LANTERN CARRIED BY THE WIND

ON THE NIGHT OF THE FESTIVAL, A
father stood at the river's edge beside his son.

All around them, families lit paper lanterns and set them afloat, watching as they drifted across the dark water, carried by the wind.

The son's hands trembled as he held his own lantern. "What if the wind takes it the wrong way?" he asked.

The father smiled. "The wind always takes things where they need to go."

Still, the boy hesitated, gripping the lantern tightly. "But I worked hard to make it perfect."

The father knelt beside him. "Then let it fly."

Slowly, reluctantly, the son released the lantern. It bobbed unsteadily in the air before catching the breeze, rising higher and higher. His eyes followed it as it floated beyond the trees, its glow becoming smaller and smaller, until at last, it disappeared into the night.

For a long time, the son said nothing. Then, finally, he smiled.

The next morning, the father stood at the gate of their home as the son prepared to leave for the city. Now grown, he adjusted the straps of his traveling pack.

"Will you be all right?" the son asked.

The father chuckled. "The wind always takes things where they need to go."

And with that, the son bowed and walked away, his figure growing smaller with each step —eventually, he disappeared into the horizon.

The father remained at the gate for a while, watching the sky.

Reflection

How does letting go create space for love to grow?

Can you trust the wind, even when you don't know where it leads?

———

A Moment of Zen

Light a candle and watch the flame dance in the air. Notice how it moves but never resists.

Stand outside and feel the wind on your skin. Ask yourself: *Where has this wind been before?*

Release a leaf or flower into a stream and watch it float. Reflect on how things find their own way.

19

THE FISHERMAN WHO STOPPED FISHING

THE OLD FISHERMAN HAD SPENT HIS
life by the river. Each morning, before the sun

touched the water, he cast his net. Each evening, he returned home with his catch, selling some, cooking some, and releasing the smallest back into the current.

One day, as he pulled in his net, he found a single fish—strong, silver, and perfect. He held it in his hands, feeling its weight, its life thrumming against his palms.

He looked at the river, then back at the fish.

For the first time, he did not think about selling it or cooking it. He did not think about keeping it at all.

Instead, he knelt by the water's edge and opened his hands. The fish hesitated for a moment, then flicked its tail and disappeared beneath the surface.

The fisherman sat there, watching the ripples fade. His net lay empty beside him.

That evening, he returned home with nothing but the scent of the river on his skin. And he felt lighter than he had in years.

The next morning, for the first time in his life, he did not bring his net to the water. He simply sat and watched the river flow.

And somehow, it was enough.

BEAUTY IN THE ZEN

Reflection

Does releasing something mean you have lost
it, or does it remain with you in another way?

What have you held onto for too long, fearing
that letting go would leave you empty?

———

A Moment of Zen

Hold a small object in your hand, then
release it.
Notice how it feels before and after.

Watch a river or the ocean.
Reflect on how it gives and takes without
hesitation.

Breathe in deeply, then exhale.
Ask yourself: *Did the breath belong to me?*

20

THE CANDLE THAT LIGHTS ANOTHER

A TRAVELER ARRIVED AT A MONASTERY late one evening, shivering from the cold. The halls were dim, lit only by a single candle flickering beside an old monk who sat in meditation.

"Master," the traveler said, bowing, "forgive my intrusion, but the road was dark, and I could not find my way."

The monk nodded. "Darkness is only the absence of light."

He took a second candle, touched it to the flame of the first, and passed it to the traveler. "Now there are two."

The traveler held the candle, its warmth spreading through his fingers. "But, Master, your own flame has not dimmed."

The old monk smiled. "That is the nature of light. It does not grow smaller when shared—it only spreads."

The traveler stared at the two flames, identical yet separate, and something in his heart stirred. Bowing once more, he left the monastery, carrying his light into the night.

As he walked through the village, he passed a beggar curled beneath a tree. Without hesitation, the traveler bent down and passed the flame to the beggar's candle.

Now there were three.

And the night seemed less dark than before.

Reflection

What in your life multiplies when you give it away?

Do you fear that sharing will leave you with less?
What if it leaves you with more?

———

A Moment of Zen

Light a candle and use it to light another. Observe how the first flame remains unchanged.

Smile at a stranger and notice if kindness echoes back to you.

Sit in the dark, then light a single candle. Ask yourself: *What else in my life can push back the darkness?*

21

THE WIND IN THE BAMBOO

A MAN BUILT A GARDEN FILLED WITH
rare and beautiful plants. But his greatest trea-

sure was a row of tall bamboo, their slender stalks swaying gracefully in the breeze.

Each morning, he stood among them, listening to the wind rustle through the leaves. The sound brought him peace, as if the wind itself were singing to him.

One day, fearing that a storm might snap the delicate stalks, he tied ropes around them, anchoring them tightly to the ground. "Now they will be safe," he thought.

That evening, the wind returned. But this time, the bamboo did not dance. It stood rigid, bound and silent.

Days passed, and the man noticed the leaves turning yellow, the stalks growing brittle. Without their freedom to bend, the bamboo was beginning to break.

Realizing his mistake, he rushed to untie the ropes. The next time the wind came, the bamboo swayed once more, moving effortlessly with the current. And the garden was filled with music again.

The man closed his eyes and smiled. He had

not protected the bamboo by holding it still—
he had only silenced its song.

Reflection

Where in your life do you try to hold
something too tightly, thinking it will keep it
safe?

What happens when love is given the space to
move freely?

———

A Moment of Zen

Stand outside and feel the wind pass over you.
Notice how it moves without grasping.

Hold your hands tightly in fists, then release
them.
Observe the difference in sensation.

Watch the trees sway in the breeze.
Ask yourself: *Do they resist?*

Message From The Author

Thank you for taking the time to read *Beauty in the Zen*. My hope is that these stories have brought you moments of stillness, clarity, or even a small shift in perspective.

This book is part of a larger journey—to share the wisdom of Zen in a simple, accessible way so that more people can experience its teachings and find peace in their lives. In a world that often feels chaotic, even a single story can be a stepping stone to stillness.

If you found value in this book, I'd appreciate it if you could leave an honest review. Your feedback helps others discover these teachings.

<u>Scan the QR Code or click here to share your thoughts.</u>

Thank you for being part of this journey.

— *Kai*

References

Kapleau, Philip. *The Three Pillars of Zen: Teaching, Practice, and Enlightenment.* New York: Anchor Books, 1989.

Morse, Mark, trans. *The Gateless Gate: The Classic Book of Zen Koans.* Berkeley: Counterpoint, 2019.

Reps, Paul, and Nyogen Senzaki. *Zen Flesh, Zen Bones: A Collection of Zen and Pre-Zen Writings.* Boston: Tuttle Publishing, 1998.

Sekida, Katsuki. *Zen Training: Methods and Philosophy.* Boston: Shambhala Publications, 2005.

Suzuki, Shunryu. *Zen Mind, Beginner's Mind.* New York: Shambhala Publications, 2006.

Watts, Alan. *The Way of Zen.* New York: Vintage Books, 1957.

Yamada, Koun. *Zen: The Authentic Gate.* Somerville, MA: Wisdom Publications, 2015.